Disney Fancy NANCY

Nancy's Ghostly Halloween

Based on the episode written by Laurie Israel
Adapted by Krista Tucker
Illustrated by the Disney Storybook Art Team

HARPER FESTIVAL

An Imprint of HarperCollinsPublishers

ISBN 978-0-06-279827-5

Typography by Brenda E. Angelilli/Scott Petrower
18 19 20 21 22 CWM 10 9 8 7 6 5 4 3 2 1 ❖ First Edition

Ooh la la! It's Halloween! I can't wait for everyone to see my fancy butterfly costume.

Bree and I are going trick-or-treating with my little sister, JoJo. JoJo's knight costume squeaks and creaks when she walks.

"Hurry, JoJo," I say.
I'm not sure what she says. Her helmet covers her face and all I hear is "Mmph, mmum, mwaa."

It's a windy and cold day, so Mom wants me to wear a coat when we go trick-or-treating.

"But Mom!" I protest. "A coat would cover my costume and that would be disastrous."

I know, I'll wear my cloak instead. It swirls
and sways to show my fabulous costume.

"Have fun," Mom says. "Nancy, keep an eye on your sister!"

"Wait for me!" shouts JoJo, lagging behind.

We're not too far when JoJo screams!

"JoJo, what's the matter?" I ask.

"Those ghosts are scary!" she says, pointing
to the trees.

"Don't worry," I tell JoJo. "I know those ghosts look real, but they're just decorations."

Suddenly, one flies right toward us!

"Ahhh!" we scream.

But the ghost is just a sheet. Whew!
There is nothing to be afraid of!

"You can't let your imagination run away with you," I tell JoJo. That's fancy for thinking something is real when it's not.

"Let's go to Mrs. Devine's," I say. "She will adore my costume."

"Trick-or-treat!" we say, ringing the doorbell.

"Bree, what a cute bunny you are," Mrs. Devine says.
"And you are a very noble knight, JoJo. And Nancy, you
are one terrific . . . flying grape?"

I whisk off my cloak. I'd rather be a cold butterfly than a flying grape.

"You dropped your cloak!" JoJo says behind me.

Bree and I hurry ahead to the next house. JoJo isn't with us. We turn back for her, but all we see is a ghost!

"Ahh!" we yell.

Even though I'm practically an expert at being calm, I start to feel afraid.

I whisk off my cloak. I'd rather be a cold butterfly than a flying grape.

"You dropped your cloak!" JoJo says behind me.

Bree and I hurry ahead to the next house. JoJo isn't with us. We turn back for her, but all we see is a ghost!

"Ahh!" we yell.

Even though I'm practically an expert at being calm, I start to feel afraid.

"Naaancy! Breeeee!" the ghost shouts.
"That is not a decoration," I tell Bree.
"That ghost knows our names!"

Bree and I are more than scared.
We are petrified!
We must escape the ghost
and find JoJo!

"Come back!" the ghost shouts.

Bree and I hide. The ghost squeaks and creaks.
It keeps coming for us.

We turn to flee and run
straight into a zombie!
"Ahhh!" we scream.

"Relax, guys," says our friend Lionel, lifting his zombie mask. "It's me!"

"We lost JoJo," I tell him. "And there's a ghost chasing us."

"Ghosts aren't real," says Lionel.
Then the ghost calls, "Liooonel!"
"It is real!" Lionel says. "Run!"

We run to my house to see if JoJo is there.
It's also a good place to hide from the ghost.
I hope JoJo is safe inside.
We hurry into the house and close the door.

"JoJo? Are you home?" I shout.

The doorknob rattles. "Let me in!" the ghost shouts.

We jump back in fright as the ghost squeaks and creaks on the other side of the door.

"Nancy!" I hear JoJo shout from outside.
"JoJo!" I am so happy to hear my sister's voice!
But she is outside with the ghost instead of
safely inside with us. I must save her!

I fling open the door.
I don't see a ghost.

But I see JoJo wearing
my cloak. I am puzzled,
which is fancy for confused!

"Were you wearing my cloak this whole time?" I ask JoJo.
"I was trying to give it back to you," JoJo explains.

"Oh JoJo, we thought you were a ghost chasing us!" I say.
Bree, Lionel, and I feel foolish, which is fancy for silly.

"Can we go trick-or-treating now?" asks JoJo.
"Oui, oui," I say. "But I should probably wear my cloak from now on." Our night of fun is just beginning!

Happy Halloween!